Tropical Paradise Scenes
to Paint or Color

Dot Barlowe

DOVER PUBLICATIONS, INC.
Mineola, New York

Note

You can almost feel the warm breeze as you page through this beautiful coloring book featuring a variety of tropical settings. These exotic islands offer us a most unusual assortment of birds, flowers, and sea life. Among the sandy beaches, palm trees, and huts you will find colorful macaws, pink flamingos, brown pelicans, and thick-billed plovers. Some of the most beautiful flowers in the world are located on these tropical islands like the hibiscus and bird-of-paradise. The secluded locations of these tropical paradises are perfect for water sports. A trip in the kayak or catamaran allows you go explore the coastline quietly so as not to disturb the fish, sea lions, dolphins, and turtles. And the massive waves are a surfer's delight. So sit back and relax in your hammock and enjoy a piece of paradise!

Watch the printed lines practically disappear as you create your own personal masterpieces using pencil, pen, paint, or any other media. The illustrations are printed on one side only on high-quality paper making them suitable for framing when completed. To remove the pages, carefully tear them out following the perforation.

Bibliographical Note

Tropical Paradise Scenes to Paint or Color is a new work, first published by Dover Publications, Inc., in 2009.

DOVER *Pictorial Archive* SERIES

This book belongs to the Dover Pictorial Archive Series. You may use the designs and illustrations for graphics and crafts applications, free and without special permission, provided that you include no more than four in the same publication or project. (For permission for additional use, please write to Permissions Department, Dover Publications, Inc., 31 East 2nd Street, Mineola, N.Y. 11501.)

However, republication or reproduction of any illustration by any other graphic service, whether it be in a book or in any other design resource, is strictly prohibited.

International Standard Book Number
ISBN-13: 978-0-486-46562-3
ISBN-10: 0-486-46562-4

Manufactured in the United States of America
Dover Publications, Inc., 31 East 2nd Street, Mineola, N.Y. 11501